A DAY IN THE LIFE OF
A BABY BEAR

BY PETER AND SUSAN BARRETT

WHISTLESTOP

Troll

A Nutshell Book

Library of Congress Cataloging-in-Publication Data

Barrett, Susan (date)
A day in the life of a baby bear / by
Susan & Peter Barrett.
p.   cm.
Summary: A little bear's first swim almost becomes a disaster when
a strong current sweeps her away from the shore.
ISBN 0-8167-3817-3 (pbk.)
1. Bears—Juvenile fiction. [1. Bears—Fiction.] I. Barrett,
Peter, ill.   II. Title.
PZ10.3.B2705Db   1996
[Fic]—dc20   95-7164

One day in the late autumn a mother bear made a den beneath the branches of a fallen birch tree. She knew winter was coming. Even her thick black fur coat could not protect her from the cold north wind. She crawled into her den, and there she slept all winter, curled up in a tight, furry ball.

There was still snow on the ground when she gave birth to twin bear cubs. The babies were tiny, no bigger than a man's hand. Their eyes were closed. They had no fur, but their mother's long, shaggy winter coat kept them warm. They fed on their mother's milk and grew a little bigger and stronger every day. Soon they opened their eyes and began to grow soft, fluffy fur.

One day the mother bear sensed a change in the air. She raised her head toward the sky and twitched her nose. She could smell the first scents of springtime: cherry blossoms, new grass, and fragrant wildflowers.

The mother bear crawled out of her winter home, followed by her cubs. The cubs squinted and blinked in the bright sunlight.

The sun shone on their fur and showed the difference between them. One baby bear had a shiny, jet-black coat, while her brother's fur was a deep chocolate brown.

At first the mother and her cubs stayed close to the den. The cubs learned about life in the forest and how to climb trees to escape danger. When a raccoon came too close, the mother bear growled a warning, and the cubs scampered up the nearest tree.

The cubs learned how to stand on their hind legs so they could see what was happening farther away.

They loved playing games, racing,
romping, and wrestling with each other.
The jet-black cub was a little smaller than
her brother, but she was quicker.

After a few months the twins were big enough to wander through the forest. They followed their mother as she looked for all the things bears like to eat: insects, grubs, plants, berries, and, best of all, fish from the streams and rivers.

One day the bears found a stream full of silvery-colored fish swimming upstream to lay their eggs. What a feast this would be! The mother bear swam out into the icy-cold stream to catch the fish. The twins stayed on the shore.

The days grew warmer, and soon it was summertime. One day, when the sun was shining brightly in a clear, blue sky, the bears returned to the stream. The cubs had grown braver since their first visit to the stream. This time, when their mother swam out into the stream, the twins followed her.

The cubs were glad to escape the biting flies and to splash about in the cool water.

The cubs were so busy playing that they didn't notice their mother had returned to the shore. She had seen a huge, black male bear at the water's edge.

She thought her cubs might be in danger, so she bared her teeth and growled loudly to scare him away.

Out in the stream the brown cub heard his mother's warning growls and swam back to the shore. His sister tried to follow him, but the current was too strong. The current began pulling her farther and farther from the shore.

The current swept the cub faster and faster downstream, carrying her toward a place where the stream joined a wide, deep river.

The water splashed about her ears, spun her in circles, and pushed her past big boulders. The cub couldn't even cry for help. All she could do was keep her nose out of the water.

When her brother reached the shore, he realized his sister wasn't with him. The two cubs had never been apart before. He let out a long, frightened howl and began running along the bank of the stream. His mother raced after him, plunged into the water, and swam out to rescue her little cub.

The baby bear saw her mother coming and yelped with joy. Her mother seized her by the scruff of her neck and lifted her out of the water. The baby bear clung to her mother's neck with all her might as her mother carried her back to shore.

There she lay in the warm sun as her mother licked
her dry and her brother stood by, waiting to play.

Soon she was on her feet again, and the
twins were doing what they enjoyed most,
romping, wrestling, and . . .

. . . chasing each other around in circles.

For the rest of that summer the baby bear stayed in the shallow water near the shore. Not even the tastiest fish could tempt her out into the stream. But by the following summer she had become a strong swimmer. She was able to swim out into the deepest waters of the stream and catch fish herself. Someday, when she had cubs of her own, she would catch fish for them, too.